Heirs
for the
Holiday

AN ORACLE M NOVELLA

EDWARD GASTON

EDWARD GASTON

Heirs for the Holidays
An Oracle M Novella
BY EDWARD GASTON

First published in the United States of America
Copyright (c) 2024 Edward Gaston
Jacksonville, Florida

ISBN 978-1-944155–38-4
Library of Congress Control Number: 2025944875

onald Potter leaned back in his leather chair, the sky-line of Jacksonville, Florida, sprawling behind him. His phone buzzed.

"Donald," came the sharp voice of his boss, Claire Barrington. "We've got a situation in Brightmoor. That heir property is a prime location for RAXY's next project. I want it closed by Christmas."

Donald smirked, "You called the right man. I've already got one heir to sell me their interest and the rest will follow."

"Good, this could add to your bonus if you get it done by Christmas." Claire's tone was matter-of-fact.

"Trust me," Donald replied, a glint of confidence in his eyes. "It's as good as done." Donald rose and walked from his office as

Santa Claus Go Straight to the Ghetto by James Brown, played in the background.

Arrival in Brightmoor was not what Donald expected. The small diverse town was alive with Christmas cheer—wreaths hung from every lamppost, storefronts glittered with lights, and carolers sang on the corner of Main Street.

"Welcome to the Brightmoor Inn," said a woman from behind the front desk, as Donald entered the boutique hotel.

Donald stopped in his tracks. She was striking—natural hair framed her face, her eyes steady and discerning.

"Deborah Jackson," she said, extending her hand, while *What Do the Lonely Do at Christmas* by Patti Labelle, flowed through the speakers.

She stood with an air of quiet confidence that seemed to command attention without effort. Her warm, rich brown skin glowed under the soft lighting of the boutique hotel she owned, complementing the earth tones of her outfit—a fitted, olive-green sweater that accentuated her curvy figure and a pair of tailored dark jeans. Her hair, a cascade of deep chestnut with hints of golden highlights, framed her oval-shaped face, falling just above her shoulders in a natural, graceful flow.

Her eyes seemed to hold stories untold, their hazel warmth invited conversation with unyielding intensity. She had a quiet smile that could disarm even the most guarded, with a natural fullness to her lips that softened the determined set of her jaw. Her high cheekbones and delicate nose gave her an elegance that was both understated and striking.

Deborah moved with purpose, her every gesture fluid yet deliberate, her posture straight but never rigid. Her voice, when she spoke, carried a smooth, melodic tone—assertive without being harsh, comforting without being overly familiar. It was the kind of voice that left an impression, making her words linger even after she'd stopped speaking.

Whether tending to guests at her hotel or navigating the Town of Brightmoor, Deborah exuded an aura of self-reliance and pride, tempered with a genuine care for others. It was this blend of strength and warmth that made her unforgettable.

"Donald Potter," he replied, giving her a practiced smile, "and you're the owner?"

"Manager and owner," she corrected. "Here for business or pleasure?"

"Business, but who says it can't be both?"

Deborah arched a brow. "Enjoy your stay." She handed him the room key and turned to help another guest, quietly dismissing Donald. He took the key and walked to his room for a little relaxation.

The Brightmoor Café was alive with holiday cheer. Strings of white lights twinkled along the windows, garlands framed the door, and the scent of cinnamon and fresh pine hung in the air. The Temptations's *Silent Night* softly played in the background, blending seamlessly with the murmur of patrons chatting over cups of steaming coffee. Myles Richardson sat at a corner table, scanning through a worn folder of documents. His brow furrowed in concentration. Myles's wardrobe often reflected his dual identity. On any given day, he might pair well-fitted denim and sturdy boots with a pressed dress shirt, the sleeves rolled up to reveal forearms that spoke of a man unafraid to get his hands dirty. When the occasion called for it, he donned sharp suits with ease, always ensuring his appearance was polished yet approachable. His tailored suits and polished demeanor revealed his confidence in the military, boardrooms, and bank offices.

On days when he needed his mind to grind through solutions, Myles wore a long-sleeve white crewneck decorated with a single, red ΚΑΨ embroidered on the left breast, and a hat bearing the same.

When the door jingled open, he glanced up, instinctively expecting just another customer. His breath caught in his throat when he saw her. He removed his hat as if doing so would improve his vision.

Carolyn.

Carolyn Dupree!

Tall, poised, and wrapped in a crimson Victorian cloak that released an aura under the cafe's golden light, she was every bit as striking as he remembered. Her presence was commanding.

"Carolyn Dupree," he said, rising from his chair. His voice a mix of disbelief and delight. Her features were striking: dark, piercing eyes that seemed to take in every detail, high cheekbones that added a regal quality, and full lips often curved into a subtle smile that hinted at both warmth and wisdom. Her skin, a rich cocoa tone, radiated a natural glow, as though lit from within. Standing six feet in Chuck Taylor's, she moved like a silent gazelle.

She stopped mid-step, "Myles!" Her dark eyes widening as a radiant smile lifted her face. "Look at you! I almost didn't recognize you without those glasses."

Myles Richardson stood tall. His broad shoulders revealed a life spent balancing the physical demands of the land with weighted accuracy of financial expertise. His hands were strong, calloused from honest labor. His face was a study in contrasts—a wide, welcoming smile often softened his sharp jaw lines and high cheekbones. His deep-set eyes, framed by a furrow of thoughtfulness, carried an intensity that suggested he saw both potential and challenges in everything. His neatly trimmed goatee added an air of maturity and complemented his low fade haircut.

Myles chuckled, smoothing his shirt self-consciously. "And I almost didn't recognize you without the basketball under your arm." His voice, a rich baritone, carried the warmth of someone deeply connected to his roots, with a cadence that was both measured and persuasive.

Carolyn's tall, statuesque frame accentuated her elegance. She had toned arms, and her long legs seemed to glide effortlessly, whether she wore sneakers or four-inch Kendall Miles. Her athletic build a testament to years of discipline and care.

"You are a welcomed sight," Carolyn said, pulling out a chair and sitting across from him. "How long has it been?" She paused and listened to the cafe's sound system switch to Nat King Cole's *The Christmas Song*. "I'm guessing, what, ten years?"

"Eleven," Myles said, settling back into his seat.

"You know," Carolyn said, stirring her coffee, "We had crazy fun as kids in this town, but, we barely talked in high school. You became so serious, like you need to save the world serious."

Myles feigned offense, raising an eyebrow. "Save the world serious? You mean 'focused and brilliant serious,' right?" Whether he was discussing crop yields with local farmers or outlining a strategic financial plan for a community project, Myles spoke with conviction and clarity. They shared a laugh, the kind that started awkwardly but quickly melted into something warm and familiar.

"Sure, let's go with that," Carolyn teased. "But then we ended up at the same college, and suddenly you weren't too serious anymore. You were...actually pretty cool."

"Cool? Coming from the campus superstar? I'll take it."

Carolyn smiled. She unfastened the silver clasps of her cloak and lifted it from her shoulders before laying it on the back of the chair. Carolyn's fashion sense was bold and confident, her wardrobe full of tailored pieces and sophisticated heels that celebrated her height and athletic frame. She knew how to pair a sharply cut blazer with slim-fit trousers or rock a form-fitting dress that exuded both power and grace.

"I remember those late-night study sessions. You'd be buried in textbooks, and I'd be trying to cram between road trips and games. How did you even put up with me?"

"Easy," Myles said with a grin. "You brought snacks. Do you have a Twix on you now? What about a pecan log?" He reached out his hand, beckoning with his fingers. Carolyn hit his hand. With a fond muscle memory, their palms clasped, fingers clinched each other's wrists then slid quickly down the palms to the tips of the fingers which retreated into two synchronistic snaps.

Their laughter drew a curious glance from the barista.

"Those were good times." Carolyn's gaze softened, her fingers traced the rim of her coffee mug. "You were always so patient, even when I'd show up half-asleep or complaining about practice."

Myles shrugged, his smile wistful. "I admired your drive. You made me want to work harder, even when I was dog-tired from ROTC."

"And then life happened." Carolyn's expression grew thoughtful, "You went off to the military, and I went overseas. It's crazy how fast time slips away."

Myles nodded, a trace of regret flickered in his chest. "I tried to stay in touch. I even called your sister a few times to get your number when I came back. But…"

Carolyn's eyebrows knit together. "Wait, what? My sister never told me you called."

"Figures," Myles said offering a wry smile. "She always did love keeping me in the dark."

Carolyn shook her head. "I'm sorry, Myles." With a tinge of nervousness, she rubbed her hands through her voluminous coils. Myles noticed how her curls feathered freely, naturally, and framed her face. Her brown, greying strands glistened healthily. It magnified her aura of authenticity and self-assurance." If I'd known, I would've called you back in a heartbeat."

For a moment, their eyes met, and the world seemed to pause. Myles felt a strange warmth spread through him.

"So," Carolyn said, breaking the silence, "what have you been up to here in Brightmoor? I heard you came back after the military."

"Yeah," Myles said, clearing his throat. Myles had a unique charisma—a grounded, unpretentious air that made him equally at home in a barn or a bank. His presence exuded a quiet leadership, the kind that inspired trust and respect in those who worked alongside him. "I came back and got roped into banking and community work. Brightmoor's got its challenges, but it's home, you know? I'm trying to make a difference, especially with the land."

Carolyn's smile faded. "I heard about that. My grandparents used to tell me stories about the farm—how it was a cornerstone for the community. What exactly is going on with it?" Her voice was low and steady, each word deliberate and clear, carrying the kind of authority that made people listen. Whether engaging in a lighthearted conversation or leading a serious discussion, Carolyn exuded a charisma that was impossible to ignore. She was a woman who understood her power and embraced it fully, inspiring those around her without even trying.

Myles sighed, his jaw tightening. "It's heir's property, which means the land's divided among family members who are descendants of the original owners. The problem is that a corporation swooped in, claiming they bought the rights from one of the heirs. Now they're trying to take the whole thing." He gestured at the papers scattered on the table.

"That's awful," Carolyn said and watched him pile the papers back into a folder. After he slid the folder under his hat and cellphone, she asked. "What can you do?" She knew him well enough to know he had a plan although she didn't want to respond with such familiarity.

"Not much I can do without getting everyone on the same page," Myles admitted. "I can't let it go. It's more than just land—it's history. It's home."

"You're doing the right thing. I know you won't give up until you figure it out."

Myles nodded, his gaze lingering on her eyes for a moment. She's still beautiful. "What about you? Will you continue coaching?"

"I don't know. I have received a few offers, but, I am going to take my time In making a decision. My last season coaching at A&M took a lot out of me," she said, with her smile returning. "It definitely has been a journey. Playing overseas was lonely sometimes—different languages, cultures, and always being on the move. But it taught me a lot, especially about managing my money. By the time I came back to the WNBA, I felt like I could handle anything. And coaching has been such a wonderful and fulfilling experience."

"No regrets?"

"None," Carolyn said firmly. "I've been blessed in so many ways. And being back here for the holidays, seeing faces like yours, it reminds me of what really matters. Like the Richardson family's good ole poundcake! Do y'all still have it and what time can an old friend stop by for half a cake?" She lifted her mug, now half full of coffee, and gave Myles a feigned toast before sipping.

Behind the laughter and nostalgia, Carolyn Dupree felt a hum silently between them—a tease of something new, or perhaps, something old rekindling in the holiday glow. After an hour, Carolyn ended their short reunion, offering to give Myles time and space to return to his work. She knew his social barometer was limited when he'd set his sights on accomplishing a task. And in that moment, she was right.

Myles was relentless in his mission to rally the Richardson family. Their 110 acres of farmland and other scattered land holdings had been more than just property, it was the soul of the family and a source for the community. It had seen decades of joy: weddings under the sprawling oak trees, reunions stretched across generations, and summer fireworks across the Alabama night sky. For Brightmoor residents, the land was a nostalgic treasure, offering hayrides and berry-picking jobs that left a mark on countless childhoods.

Myles woke to a humid-cold snap that December brings to Brightmoor. From dawn until nine, the morning air smelled like the frost trapped in his grandmother's freezer. Myles stood at the door of the Richardson family home, taking in deep breaths, to welcome the day.

The home was a sprawling, creamy-white two-story farmhouse set atop a gentle hill overlooking the family's acreage. Built with ancestral sweat and skill, it bore the Richardson's air of rustic elegance and resilience.

Dark green shutters framed each of the nine wide-paneled windows. A wraparound porch stretched eight-feet into the yard. Myles adjusted the creaky wooden swing and several rocking chairs, knowing family would soon gather, catch up on gossip, and watch sunsets. The porch railings, painted a matching green, were adorned with climbing vines of jasmine, their fragrant blooms still lingered in December. He walked the perimeter of the porch, surprised to see a large vegetable garden sat to one side, with rows of collards, sweet potatoes, and okra. A chicken coop, worn with age, was east of the garden. A dozen hens clucked quietly, foraging, and feeding in the morning sun. Beyond the ancient oak trees that shaded the yard, Myles could see a barn with loose hay, a rusted tractor, a flat boat, and a small tool shed—reminders of his family's agricultural roots.

He stood acknowledging the majesty of this land.

Myles returned inside. The house was a warm blend of history and comfort. The hardwood floors, worn in places, spoke to the many feet that had walked there over the decades.The home wasn't perfect—it had its creaks and drafts, and the paint needed touching up in places—but it was the embodiment of the Richardson family's legacy. It was more than just a house; it was a living archive of their struggles, triumphs, and deep-rooted connection to the land. It was home to many.

With the discernment of a contractor, Myles noticed the wide entryway and its staircase with a banister polished smooth by four generations of hands. To the left was the formal sitting room, where family heirlooms filled shelves and old portraits hung in ornate frames.

He entered the large kitchen, remembering how it smelled perpetually of something delicious—whether it was Cousin Mamie's pound cake, Aunt Nadine's biscuits, or a pot of collard greens simmering on the stove. The kitchen walls were lined with open shelves holding mason jars filled with dried goods, spices, moonshine, and preserves, alongside mismatched ceramic plates that had been collected over time.

After a small breakfast of toast and eggs, Myles left to visit the elders of the family: Great-Aunt Sharon, a retired schoolteacher with a steely glare that could silence a room, and Great Uncle

Philip, whose hands were so calloused from years of farming now only held a fishing pole.

In their cozy living room, surrounded by shelves of books and walls holding faded family photos, Myles finished explaining his plan.

"What makes you think this Mission More group can help us?" Great Uncle Philip asked, leaning forward in his armchair.

"We've managed this land as is for decades. Now you're talking about bringing in outsiders to tell us how to divide it up? I still have life in me."

"They're not outsiders," Myles replied, his tone calm but firm. "Mission More is a nonprofit that specializes in helping families and communities like ours. They'll give us the tools to keep the land in the family and develop it for generational wealth. Without them, we will have a tough time against RAXY."

Great Aunt Sharon studied him over the rim of her teacup. "You've always been determined, Myles. You get that from your grandfather. I'll come to the meeting, but don't expect me to sugarcoat or outright agree to any thing."

Great Uncle Philip nodded. "I'll listen. But I'm not making any promises either," he said grudgingly, as he walked Myles to the door. The elders had a peculiar way of ending conversations and reclaiming their space. Before Myles could say a decent goodbye, his great relatives had closed the door and returned to their day's work. Myles was proud of their willingness to meet, although he knew the out-of-town and younger relatives posed a greater challenge.

~~ ~~

That evening, Myles's sisters, Diane and Phylicia, arrived from Atlanta. They marveled at the living room's oversized stone fireplace, remembering nights they snuggled together on the overstuffed couches sharing the hand-stitched quilts that were still draped over armrests. Both of them touched the family photos lining the mantelpiece.

"These pictures chronicle everything from weddings to Sunday afternoons on the porch," Phylicia acknowledged. Upstairs, the bedrooms bore layers of history, from faded wallpaper to the faint pencil marks measuring children's heights over the years.

After they removed their coats and unloaded their suitcases, the sisters met Myles in the kitchen.

"Myles, are you cooking that tired chicken and potatoes?" Diane teased.

"I sure am. So get your palate ready for some good eating unlike those salads and smoothies you've been posting on Facebook," Myles tease.

"Leave my brother's cooking alone," Phylicia joined in, laughing. "He's the best, sober male cook of the family." She hugged Myles. "You're looking good brother and the food smells great."

Diane opened three cabinet doors before she found plates and glasses. She rinsed and wiped the plates clean before fixing their meals. "Well, sir, we are here earlier as you asked. Are you ready to tell us what's happening in the big town of Brightmoor that the entire Richardson clan needed to be here for the holidays?" She said.

In the dining room, the three siblings sat at a massive oak farmhouse table, with twelve wooden seats. An antique chandelier cast a warm glow as the sunset early. At the opposite end of the table, Myles already placed note cards, pencils, yellow note pads, an architect's scale, a large plat map, and documents printed on blue legal paper.

Their skepticism palpable. Diane, a public defender, wasted no time attempting to dissect the legal aspects of the land dispute, while Phylicia, an accountant, focused on the financial implications.

"This could end up being a money pit," Phylicia said during dinner, her fork paused mid-air. "We need to think about the longterm risks."

"It's not just about money," Myles countered. Patience leveled his voice. "This land is part of who we are. It's part of who Mom and Dad were. It's Richardson through three generations. We are the fourth. Do you really want to let that go?"

For each of them, that legacy carried unspoken meanings,

Diane leaned back in her chair. Her expression thoughtful. "I'm not saying I want to let it go, Myles. But we need to approach this strategically. If RAXY has partial rights, and I truly can't tell from looking at these documents, then, we need to figure out who sold to them and why." They all considered faces of aunts, cousins, uncles, and their known offspring.

Diane cut three slices of poundcake and gave one to each of her siblings. They took their first bites in silence, lost in the lingering questions and adoring the familiar taste of their family recipe. "This is the best pound cake ever. Nothing better than Cousin Mamie's pound cake." Phylicia said. "I need this recipe!"

There was a knock at the door.

Diane answered the door and announced Tara and Laina, their cousins, had arrived. After giving them a quick overview and sharing concerns, Myles realized their arrival added tension. Tara, a real estate broker, was intrigued by RAXY's aggression and suggested the family take time to listen to the company's plans and give a counter offer.

Laina, an artist, vehemently opposed the idea. "This land has soul," Laina argued, her hands gesturing animatedly. "Our land has soul," her voice rose with passion. "You can't just put a price tag on something like that."

"And soul doesn't pay the bills," Tara shot back.

"Tara." Myles said, his tone authoritative. "We're not going to figure this out by arguing. We will work together, or we'll lose this land and our legacy piece by piece."

Laina nodded. Tara groaned, "Fine with me. Let me get a piece of that poundcake."

"It is delicious." Phylicia chimed in from the kitchen.

~~ ~~

Sounds of Christmas flowed in every space around the Town of Brightmoor. Donny Hathaway crooned This Christmas in the foyer of the Mahone Library. Walking through the corridor heading to the back meeting room, Donald hummed the chorus as he passed the librarian.

The first time Donald stepped into Mamie Ross's presence, he was struck by her glow. The room had special furnishings and seemed to be dedicated to a prominent Brightmoor resident. A crocheted blanket draped over a dated couch, framed photos adorned the walls, and the scent of lavender lingered in the air. It was a sharp contrast to the sterile, high-rise offices of RAXY Corporation.

Mamie greeted him with a warm smile. "Come on in, Mr. Potter. I have you a cup of tea."

"Please, call me Donald," he said, slipping off his coat, "Thanks for agreeing to meet. Are we allowed to drink in here?"

She nodded, "Yes. They tend to allow me to do whatever I want."

Mamie sat two steaming cups on the small table and gestured for Donald to sit. "So, you've come all the way to Brightmoor to buy land from my family."

Donald hesitated. "That's one way to put it. I see it as helping everyone get what they deserve. This land is valuable, but it is heir's property and not being used to its full potential." Donald paused. He could hear Whitney Houston singing *Joy to the World* through the library speaker. He made a mental note that the back meeting room was not soundproof, therefore, not private or safe as far as he was concerned.

Mamie stirred her tea with slow and deliberate movements. "And you think my selling of this land to your company is the progressive answer?"

"It's an opportunity," Donald said firmly. "One most people would kill for. I didn't have opportunities like this growing up."

Mamie looked up, her eyes kind but steady. "Tell me about that."

Donald positioned himself and smiled at her request, "Sure, I will get right into it. RAXY Corporation is a land developer that focuses on the southeast."

Mamie interrupted him. "Not about RAXY. I want you to tell me about you. Tell me about the opportunities that you did not have growing up."

Donald took a sip of tea, the warmth grounding him. "I was raised by a single mom. We didn't have much. No handouts, no family safety net. I worked hard—scholarships, part-time jobs, climbing the corporate ladder. I made it on my own. No one handed me anything."

He became annoyed at the nonstop playlist now running Fantasia's *I Believe*—only a bit louder.

Mamie tilted her head, her voice soft. "No one? Not a single teacher? A neighbor? A stranger who gave you a break?"

Donald frowned. "I mean...sure, maybe a few people helped along the way, but I did the work. I earned every bit of my success."

Mamie nodded thoughtfully. "I don't doubt you worked hard, Donald, but sometimes, when we look back, we miss the little gifts people gave us, a word of encouragement, a meal when we needed it, someone believing in us when we couldn't believe in ourselves."

He set the tea cup on the table a little harder than he intended. "Look, I know what people think of me. They call me a wealth stripper, say I come into communities and take what doesn't belong to me, but they don't see the bigger picture. This is business. It's not personal."

Mamie smiled gently, "But it is personal, especially to the people who live here, to families like ours. You can't separate the land from the people—it's part of who we are."

Donald's jaw tightened, "With all due respect, Mamie, not everyone clings to the past. Some of us have to move forward to survive. Progress is necessary."

"And some of us know how to carry the past with us, so we don't lose ourselves in the process," Mamie said softly, though her words landed heavily. He shifted uncomfortably. "You're not going to guilt me into thinking what I do is wrong. I've worked too hard for that to matter."

Mamie reached across the table, placing a hand lightly on his. "I'm not here to judge you, Donald. You've done what you believed you needed to do. But the universe has a funny way of showing us truth when we're ready to see it."

Donald pulled his hand back, uneasy. "Truth? Like what?"

"Like the fact that we're never as alone in our journey as we think we are. Or that, sometimes, what we're chasing isn't what we truly need."

"You sound like one of those self-help books."

Mamie chuckled, "Maybe, but I lived long enough to see how things come full circle. We can fight it, or we can embrace it." She poured herself another cup of tea from the kettle that seemed never to empty.

For a moment, only the faint ticking of a wall clock filled the room. Even the Christmas music had stopped. Donald cleared his throat. "So, Ms. Mamie Ross, are you willing to embrace progress and consider selling your interest in the land, so that we may acquire more?"

"I think I am in the place where peaceful transition is welcomed. I don't mind embracing progress." Mamie gave him a knowing smile. "How about you join my family at the main house on Christmas Eve around three p.m. to make an announcement. Then, you can validate the magnitude of the Richardson legacy."

Donald thought, *Finally looks like the deal will be made.* He nodded stiffly and stood. "Thanks for the tea and thank you for understanding what I do."

As he walked out the door, Mamie's voice followed. "Keep your heart open, Donald, you might be surprised at what finds its way in."

He paused in the doorway, her words echoed in his mind. Shaking his head, he muttered, "I don't need surprises. I need results." But deep down, a small part of him wondered if Mamie was right.

~~ ~~

Myles added working with his family to his critical office tasks because he wanted a resolution on the land before Christmas. The house phone rung loudly with the most archaic ringing. Myles chuckled at how the intrusive sound had startled him. He walked in the living room and found the landline phone resting on a wooden end table. It hadn't been moved nor the services disconnected. He cleared his throat and answered, "Good morning."

Carolyn Dupree's "Good morning, Myles. How are you?" surprised him.

"Carolyn?" He asked.

"Yes. I wanted to catch you before you left the house." She smiled knowing he was surprised that she remembered the family's phone number as much as he was glad to hear her voice. "I believe you have been carrying the weight of your family on your shoulders," she paused. "It's time for a break."

Myles hesitated. He had work to do and very little time to accomplish any of it, especially if he gave Carolyn Dupree his attention.

"A moment with an outlier may help validate your next move," she said convincingly. Myles agreed and said he would meet her after he'd tackled a few critical tasks at his office.

That evening, Carolyn took him to a quiet spot on the shore of Lewis Smith Lake, a place she remembered fondly from her childhood visits. They sat by the water, the cold breeze carrying the scent of loblolly pine and the faint sound of water moving.

"This place hasn't changed much," Carolyn said, gazing at the moonlit water.

Myles leaned back on his elbows, letting the tension in his shoulders ease. "Sometimes you can forget how peaceful peace is."

Carolyn nudged him playfully. "See? You're already relaxing."

Her laughter was infectious, and for the first time in days, Myles felt the weight of the land dispute lift. He looked at Carolyn and said, "Lets do something together again tomorrow. I'll be preparing for the representative from Mission More, but come by the house. You'd be surprise how it looks."

Carolyn smiled and responded, "Ok. I will bring the snacks."

"You better," Myles quipped.

~~ ~~

Carolyn spent more time with Myles and found herself more deeply entwined in the Richardson family. Her sister, Cecilia, who arrived to Brightmoor to spend time with Carolyn at their family home was quick to notice Carolyn's growing closeness to Myles.

"You've been spending a lot of time with Mr. Richardson," Cecilia teased one afternoon, a mischievous smile playing on her lips. "I wouldn't blame you. He's got that whole 'strong and dependable' thing going on."

"Stop it, CeCe," Carolyn said, though a faint smile crept into her face, raising an eyebrow.

"Hey, I'm just saying, you two make a good team, and who knows? Maybe you're the reason he's smiling more these days."

Carolyn couldn't help but smile more herself, thinking back to their shared moments: the laughter, the quiet conversations, the way his eyes lit up when she encouraged him. Carolyn quickly turned up Pandora to better hear "Let it Snow" by Boyz II Men. Instantly, she hummed and swayed to one song that brought back high school memories. "You know what, CeCe? I think we can help Myles and his family."

CeCe smirked. "Are you asking me to help you get your man?"

Carolyn shook her head. "Just be ready to roll with me in about hour. "

CeCe took the handle of her luggage and headed towards her bedroom.

"And!" Carolyn shouted. "In the future if a man—specifically a man named Myles Antonio Richardson— ever calls you trying to reach me, please let me know."

"Girl, what are you talking about?" CeCe laughed, nodding in agreement.

Carolyn and CeCe arrived at the county courthouse, a stoic, brick building whose faded façade spoke of its long history. The air smelled faintly of polished wood and old paper, a stark contrast to the gentle FORVR MOOD fragrances the sisters wore. Their footsteps echoed on the marble floors as they walked past portraits of stoic judges, plaques honoring Alabama's civic milestones, and a fresh cut Christmas fir decorated with white and red ribbons. Rows of neatly arranged file cabinets lined the walls, interspersed with desks where clerks worked quietly under the hum of fluorescent lights.

"I forgot how official places like this feel," CeCe whispered, glancing around.

"It's like time traveling and sleuthing." Carolyn smirked, her curiosity getting the best of her. "Well, let's see how much these archives hold beyond old white men's dealings. We need something concrete and even historic to challenge RAXY."

As they approached the far end of the room, an older, friendly-looking man wearing silver, wire-rimmed glasses, greeted them. "Good afternoon, ladies. What can I help you with today?"

"We're looking for land records, maybe deeds, liens, acquisitions, mortgages, or even conveyance," Carolyn explained. "It's the Richardson property, originally purchased by Benjamin and Etta Richardson, over in Genwea Crossing near Red Clay Road."

The clerk raised an eyebrow. "Ah, I'm very familiar with the Richardson estates. I remember hearing stories about that place all my life. Hold on. Let me check the system." As he typed into what must have been the original Tandy 2000 personal computer, Carolyn and CeCe carefully exchanged glances. Neither of them liked the way he said "estates".

"Here we are," the clerk said. "Looks like there's quite a bit in the archives. You'll want to take a look at this." The women followed him through a maze of bookshelves stacked with boxes and minute books from across the county. Dust floated between the books and shelves, but with a careful hand he followed the numbered boxes and extracted four books from three of them. He handed them to the Dupree sisters, then led them to a quiet corner where they could review the documents. "Because of the dates on some of these documents, we ask that patrons use these gloves and handle the pages with care and deliberation. If you prefer, I can assist you."

"No, sir, I believe we can handle it from here," Carolyn anxiously responded, taking the gloves he offered. CeCe noticed the glint of excitement in her sister's eyes and proudly sat across her at the wooden table. Carolyn scanned the first few pages, her eyes lighting up. "This shows the original property boundaries, which are larger than what RAXY is claiming. And here—look at this clause," she said, pointing to a line in the document. Sliding the large, brown ledger to her sister, Carolyn followed her intuition and snatched her iPhone from her inside jacket pocket and took several photographs of the pages being sure to get dates, page numbers, and close up photos of each document. Noticing the clerk watching them, Carolyn tried her best to contain her voice to a whisper. "I'm no attorney or realtor but I'm pretty sure this means that no individual family member could have sold their rights without the consent of the entire family."

CeCe leaned closer. Her detailed eye catching an old seal stamped on one of the pages. "This looks official enough to give RAXY some headaches. Do you think it'll be enough?"

"It's a start," Carolyn said, determination sharpening her voice. "I'll bring this to Myles tonight."

~~ ~~

Malcolm Wesley had a smooth, confident walk. When he entered the foyer of the Richardson home, Myles greeted him with a close-to-the-body Kappa greeting and pat on the back. His Mission More embroidered blazer fit him perfectly as far as the women who watched from the living room were concerned. His presence commanded the space and his skin browned under the warm lighting.

"That brother is sharp!" Laina whispered to no one and everyone. Sipping from a cup of warm peppermint tea, she couldn't help but notice his fresh haircut, polished, professional appearance, broad smile, and determined eyes as Myles led him into the living room.

Myles pointed to each of them as an introduction for Malcolm. "Malcom, these are our elders Grand Aunt Sharon, Aunt Nadine, and Grand Uncle Philip; my sisters Diane and Phylicia; my cousins Tara, Laina, and Aaron. CeCe and Carolyn Dupree are neighbors and family friends." Myles eyes stayed on Carolyn's until she shyly shifted her eyes. "My brothers-in-law, Kent and Lonnie, are en route. Everyone, this is Malcolm Wesley from Mission More. He's the man with the plan and all the strategies we need to succeed in the next week or so. Right, Malcolm?"

"That's right," Malcolm smiled at each of them

"Well. Hello," Laina murmured under her breath, her gaze lingering.

Carolyn leaned over and whispered, "Down, girl."

Laina shot her a playful glare and whispered. "I'm just appreciating the view. Is that a crime?" When her eyes landed on the silver wedding band, her shoulders slumped. "Psht. Never mind," she muttered, shaking her head. She grabbed the television remote, pointed it to the television just over Malcolms shoulder, to minimize the volume of Whitney Houston swooning *Do You Hear What I Hear*.

Malcolm cleared his throat, addressing everyone with a steady, reassuring voice. "Thank you all for inviting me here. I know tensions are high, but I want you to know that Mission More is here to support you. This land is more than just acreage; it's a legacy, a foundation for community strength and development."

Grand Uncle Philip leaned forward, skeptical as ever. "What exactly can you do for us, Mr. Wesley? We've heard a lot of big talk from outsiders before."

Malcolm smiled, unflustered. "Fair question, Mr. Richardson. Mission More specializes in creating pathways to keep land in family hands while making it work for the community. With our right plan, this land can be protected, developed as generational wealth, and turned into a resource that benefits both your family and Brightmoor."

Diane, always the lawyer, crossed her arms. "And how exactly do you plan to fight RAXY? They've already got their claws in part of this property and time isn't on outside with the Christmas Holiday right around the corner."

Malcolm's expression turned serious. "Yes, it seems that they have. I call their tactics 'Wealth Stripping' and we've dealt with this before. So much of these strategies of corporations like RAXY are historical and systemic. I've reviewed RAXY's preliminary reports, and I believe there are methods to deter their claim."

The family murmured.

Laina spoke first. "You talk a good game, Mr. Wesley." A mischievous glint brightened in her eye, "But let's see if you can back it up."

Malcolm chuckled, meeting her gaze. "Fair enough. And please, call me Malcolm."

Diane interrupted, "Malcolm, organizations come in and tell us the benefits of probating the heirs property with visions of wealth. Then after the land titles are cleared, we come to you and your companies for assistance and funding to develop the land and then you tell us that we don't meet your grant or loan thresholds and that we need a wealthy group or person as a partner, sending us right back to the people that were making offers to us in the first place!"

"And, it seems like RAXY has us by the neck with their million-dollar terms," said Myles.

Aunt Nadine whispered, "Aww suki suki. This is about to get good! I'm going to get me a piece of that pound cake. It looks just like the cake Cousin Mamie made."

She walks between Malcolm and Myles with a confidence astute only for a family matriarch and a sway far too young. From the dinning room table, she could be heard cutting the cake. "Oh, my goodness, this is Cousin Mamie's cake, alright! Any of ya'll want a slice?"

No one responded as she returned carrying the pound cake on a floral platter, matching saucers, forks and knife for others to enjoy. "Sit on down son," She told Malcolm, "You have our attention now."

Malcolm thought about what Diane shared and decided to change his approach. "Allow me to first explain that Mission More is supported by the Housing Assistance Council, National Association of Minority Contractors, Enterprise Foundation, LISC, NeighborWorks, J.P. Morgan Chase, along with CDFIs and community-minded banks," he said.

Diane was unimpressed as were the others; only Myles seemed to recognized the value of it.

"I know you are wondering if this kind of thing really works—if turning family land into a source of wealth instead of a source of conflict is really possible. I wondered the same thing many years ago, back when we faced a similar situation with our family property outside Tuskegee."

He unbuttoned his blazer and sat in the nearest chair. He placed his messenger bag on the floor a few feet from the grand Christmas Tree. For a moment he remembered playing the role of Santa at his own family gathering when the Wesley family discovered they had secured full ownership of the land after a lengthy fight.

"Diane, yes, I agree with your statement about probating heir property. It should only be done with a longterm plan for development."

He paused, expecting a rebuttal, not hearing one, he touched his chest and said. "I assist families with creating true generational wealth. Probating land is just part of the process. Mission More is extremely clear with our funders. All money is not good money, so if they are not on board with extending capital to assist families with land development, they are not considered full partners."

Myles began pacing slowly, his hands clasped behind his back. "Malcolm, why don't you tell us more about your family's experience. When was it? Did you have more than twelve days to respond? Where are you all with the process now?" Before he could go through more questions, Phylicia interrupted. "Those are great questions, Myles." She gave her brother a knowing look to temper his rapid-fire. "Malcolm, would you like something to drink while you answer them?"

"Sure, Phylicia, thank you." Malcolm smiled. "My family's land has about eighty acres just outside of Tuskegee, Alabama, over in Macon County. It's been in the family for about three generations, but for most of my life, it sat there, unused and under-appreciated. I'm talking about fertile land, amazing trees, fresh air, uncharted, waiting for us. My cousins and I grew up hearing the same arguments you're having now—what to do with it, who was paying the taxes, and whether we should just sell it off and be done with it."

He paused and scanned their faces. Phylicia returned with a mug of warm egg-nog stirred with cinnamon bark. *Damn, this smells good* he thought before taking the first sip. The way his head shifted, Phylicia knew he enjoyed it. She winked at Grand Aunt Sharon who had finally disclosed the family recipe only to her and the baby she was secretly expecting.

Malcolm Wesley continued. "Then, all seven of us got a wake-up call. My oldest cousins decided to sell their share to an outsider, a developer who wanted to fence the land off for private hunting and to sell most of the soil. That land wasn't just dirt to us. It was family. It was history. It was where my grandparents grew their first crops after leaving sharecropping behind. We couldn't let it go."

Malcolm leaned on the edge of a chair, his posture casual but his tone serious. "We knew we needed a plan, so we brought everyone together—just like you're doing now. We decided to form a family limited liability company to consolidate ownership and protect the land. It wasn't easy. Some folks didn't trust the idea, and others just wanted their cash. But we worked through it, with help from an attorney who explained how the L.L.C could be flexible enough to accommodate everyone's needs."

"What kind of flexibility?" asked Grand Uncle Philip, leaning forward with interest.

"For one thing," Malcolm explained, "it allowed family members who wanted out to sell their shares back to the L.L.C not to outsiders. And for those of us who stayed, it let us make decisions together without anyone feeling left out or overruled. Every member has a vote proportional to their ownership, but we agreed to a supermajority rule for major decisions. That way, no one branch of the family tree could dominate."

Malcolm continued, his voice warming as he got to the good part, "Once we had the L.L.C. in place, we started dreaming big. One cousin, an architect, suggested turning part of the land into a retreat space for corporate events and family reunions. Another, who's a horticulturist, wanted to experiment with high-tech specialty crops like saffron and mushrooms that could fetch high prices in niche markets. We went round around with the most creative concepts that we could deliver among ourselves and setting up the L.L.C. gave us the freedom to do so. It took us about four years and it has been remarkable."

He nodded at Myles and Grand Uncle Phillip, smiling. "We even installed solar panels on some of the land, turning it into a renewable energy hub that serves the community. The revenue from it alone covers the property taxes and then some. And the retreat center? It's booked solid every summer. We even get families coming in from the Midwest because they've heard about the peace and beauty of the place."

The room was silent as Malcolm's story sank in.

"And everybody in the family agreed to all that?" Grand Aunt Sharon was curious.

"Not at first," Malcolm admitted. "There were plenty of arguments along the way. But what kept us going was the idea that this land could be so much more than a burden! It could be a blessing. Now, even the cousins who sold their shares come back for reunions, and they're proud of what we've built. It's not perfect, but it's damn close."

Grand Uncle Phillip chuckled. "Sounds like you all had to put in a lot of work to make it happen."

"We did," Malcolm said, nodding. "But that's the point. Anything worth having takes effort. The question isn't whether it's easy. It's whether it's worth it."

He looked at Laina who was caught in her own imagination. "There's a lot of beauty in this family and so much untapped potential between you all."

Aaron, the youngest of the family, stood up. His fifteen-year-old face lit with excitement. "I think it's worth it! We could do something crazy, amazing here, something that honors the land and our family—especial Grandaddy Richardson!"

His enthusiasm rippled through the room, softening some of the more skeptical expressions.

Malcolm smiled at Aaron, then looked at Laina who was caught in her own imagination. "There's a lot of beauty in this family and so much untapped potential blended within you all. And it is excellent that you included Aaron. It is never too early for them to take a lead in understanding economics and wealth."

Malcolm stood up and shook the teenager's outstretched hand.

Myles place his hand on Malcolm's shoulder. "Thank you, Malcolm. Your family shows us what's possible when we come together with a shared conviction to keep our inheritance. And you're right—this won't be easy. But imagine what we could create here. Imagine what this land could mean for the next generation."

As the family murmured and began discussing among themselves, some walked into the kitchen to fix dinner and drinks. They knew there was still work to do, but Malcolm's story had planted a seed of possibility. And sometimes, a seed is all it takes to grow something extraordinary.

Myles and Carolyn exchanged glances.

CeCe gently nudged Carolyn. "Tell him about the information we found at the courthouse. I'll fix our plates." From the kitchen, she watched Myles's reaction to Carolyn showing the pages she'd scanned into her phone. She knew her sister would offer to explain it all to the family if he preferred and that the Dupree's would be by their side. Tara helped Grand Aunt Sharon and Grand Uncle Philip get comfortable as Laina prepared their plates. Kent and Lonnie arrived carrying boxes of Christmas gifts that they positioned around the tree. Lonnie pulled a broken stem of jasmine from his inner vest and asked Diane for a kiss under the feigned mistletoe. Her laughter and their kiss warmed Myles's heart. Myles prayed for his sister to have a love of a lifetime, and so far Lonnie was the one.

Once everyone was seated, the Richardson patriarch led grace, "Father God, we thank you for the food, family, and friends gathered tonight in the Richardson home. We thank you for this meal and we thank you in advance for the guidance only you can give. Lord, we are yet unsure but Your way is perfect and on this, your special holiday season, we thank You for the land that is still ours and the resources it has brought us. Let this food nourish our bodies and our minds to do what is right in your sight. This we ask in Jesus name, Amen and Amen."

As they ate, Myles caught Carolyn's eye from across the dinner table. For a moment, the joy of Christmas began to fill the room with conversations on memories, Phylicia's surprise gift for Kent, and Tara and Laina humming *Oh Holy Night* along with the Samara Joy on the stereo. Even Grand Aunt Sharon had a new smile as she sat wrapped in a patch quilt enjoying more cake. Myles felt a flicker of hope—and gratitude—for the rekindled support of the woman whose presence steadied him in the storm.

"Let's call it a night, everyone, and tomorrow we can shift to strategies and timelines, if that's okay with you Malcolm," Myles said. Everyone agreed.

"Peeerrfect!" Aaron exclaimed.

"Aaron!" Yelled Laina ready to fuss at her nephew.

"What?! Cousin Myles, promised to take me to the Lighting of the Tree at eight o'clock. I'm testing the Red Tails Squadron new drone live stream. This is perfect timing!"

"It is perfect timing," CeCe offered quickly. "Because now, I can make a grand excuse of not having to go Downtown for the shenanigans. Carolyn, why don't you join Myles, Aaron, and the Red Tails. I'll meet you at home after I've had my share of these crazy carolers!"

Aaron ran to the door and got Carolyn's coat. As he helped her put it on, Myles and Malcolm said goodnight.

~~~~~

For hours the next day, Myles and Aaron replayed the drone footage of the tree lighting and relived the beauty of lights and candle flames from a new angle. "These are great, nephew," Myles said, patting the young boy on his shoulder.

"This is new age, Cuz'! There is so much we can do."

"What do you mean?" Myles quizzed.

"Let me show you," Aaron walked over to wall television and adjusted the drone cords. "This is the Dji Phantom four Pro version two." He spoke proudly of his equipment. "And this is what it caught above the Richardson estates, sir." As if on cue, the video showed the drone's ascending to the north tip of the house. The roof was pitched steeply, covered in weathered tin that gleamed in the sunlight and sparkled softly in the rain. A hand-hewn brick chimney rose proudly on one side. It often exhaled smoke from the living room fireplace during colder months. Atop the house, the widow's walk was first visible through Aaron's video that opened to a panoramic view of the rolling fields, dense woods, and the nearby creek that weaved through the property. Myles had forgotten about the creek and the herbs and wild blackberries that grew around the bend. The drone footage gave added value and confirmed Myles's conviction to ward off RAXY and any other Wealth Strippers—as Malcolm had called them.

After lunch, the family returned to their planning session, paired off in different parts of the family room, foyer, and small office where Great Granddaddy Richardson would hold piano lessons until his death in 1909. Malcolm, Myles, Lonnie, Kent, and Aaron took charge of moving furniture so everyone could gather in one space. Among the women, Tara was most uncomfortable.

Since childhood, the Christmas holiday had always been the most stressful time of her year. This family negotiations seemed to heighten her frustrations although her inner peace had matured to settled her fray.

A knock at the door interrupted them. Laina, who was closest to the door, opened it to find a sharply dressed man standing on the porch. The stranger wore a casual buttoned shirt with RAXY embroidered in bright red. He held a sleek black briefcase.

"Good afternoon," he said smoothly, extending his hand. Laina found his smile overly lustful. "Donald Potter, representative for RAXY Corporation. I believe I have some business to discuss with your family."

Laina crossed her arms, not taking his hand. "What kind of business?"

Donald's smile didn't falter. "Land development, of course. I've been speaking to property owners in the area about exciting op-portunities, and your family's land is uniquely positioned for a major project. I'd love to explain the details if you'll allow me."

Malcolm walked over to the door. He stood a foot taller than Laina and in Donald's direct view. "I'd hate for you all to miss out on what I'm offering. With the right agreement, your family could walk away with a substantial sum. Enough to do whatever you want—move to the city, travel the world, you name it. Why struggle to keep this land when it could set you free?" Donald explained.

"You're talkin' about pennies on the dollar, aren't you?" Malcolm said. His voice vibrated in Laina's ear. *My God, this man's voice is divine.* She held her stance and watched Donald hesitate.

"Not at all," he said, his smile tightened. "RAXY Corporation believes in fair market value, and we're prepared to make a generous offer, In fact, you all should have—."

Malcolm interrupted.. "Fair market value according to who? We've heard about RAXY's projects—clear-cutting land, leaving behind environmental messes, and hiking up property taxes on the neighbors until they're forced out."

For a moment Donald's composure faltered, but he quickly recovered. "I assure you, our projects are transformative for communities. Brightmoor would benefit immensely from—" Donald coughed and cleared his throat. He attempted to look into the house and account for who may be listening. He especially needed to see if Mamie had arrived. "If you'd take a moment we can discuss your hesitations. But I'd hate for the family to miss an opportunity because of misinformation. I could sit down with everyone and go over the numbers—"

Laina held up a hand. "You've said enough. We're not interested."

As Malcolm moved to close the door, Donald raised his voice. "I wouldn't dismiss this so quickly! The legal complexities of heir property can make holding onto it challenging. Are you prepared to navigate all that without help?"

His words hit a mark. A flicker of doubt crossed some of the family members' faces. Diane, however, stepped forward, her eyes flashing.

"Thank you for your concern, Mr. Potter," her tone saccharine. "But we're more than capable of managing our own affairs. If we need legal advice, we'll call someone we trust—not a corporation looking to line its pockets."

Donald tilted his head. "Very well. But, if anyone changes their mind, I'll be in town for the next few days. Here's my card." He set a crisp business card on entry way table, then tipped his hat. "Happy holidays. And might I add, that sweet vanilla smells like a delicious dessert. Enjoy a piece or two for me."

As he strode back to his shiny black car, Malcolm muttered, "That man's got more nerve than a salvaging raccoon." He closed the door and locked it.

Laina picked up the card and inspected it before tossing it onto the coffee table in their midst. "We need to keep an eye out for people like him. They prey on families who don't know their options."

Myles nodded. "We'll stick together, like always. And make sure no one is remotely tempted by his quick cash offers."

Carolyn walked to the picture window as the sun begin to set behind Donald's car. Although the house was comfortable, the sound of *Snowflakes of Love* playing sent a shiver through her. Myles touched her shoulder.

"Do you think he'll come back?" Carolyn asked softly.

"He'll try," Myles replied. "But, so will we. We will protect and keep this land."

Carolyn smiled, slipping her hand into his. "I know you will."

~~ ~~

Donald Potter returned to the Brightmoor Inn. The warm smell of roasted turkey and cinnamon wafted through the small dining room, but it was the sight of Deborah Jackson, seated at a corner table with her laptop open, that caught his attention.

She had a slight frown on her face, her fingers clicking furiously at the keyboard.

"Mind if I join?" Donald asked, sliding into the seat across from her before she could respond.

"Yes, actually, I do," Deborah said, not even looking up.

Donald chuckled, leaning back in his chair. "Tough crowd. You always this friendly to paying guests?"

Deborah sighed, closing her laptop with a sharp snap. "What do you want, Mr. Potter?"

"For starters, for you to call me Donald," he said, grinning.

Her eyes narrowed. "Fine. What do you want, Donald?"

"To eat," he said, motioning for the server. "And maybe some company while I do. But judging by your disposition, I'd guess you've got bigger problems." He nodded at the closed laptop. "What's got you so worked up?"

"Nothing you need to worry about," Deborah said, crossing her arms.

"Humor me," Donald pressed. "I'm surprisingly helpful. You wouldn't believe it, but I once set up a full server system for a property we acquired."

Deborah raised an eyebrow. "You? A network server system?"

"Okay, fine," Donald admitted. "I called tech support. But I watched them like a hawk and learned a thing or two."

Deborah sighed, clearly debating whether to let him in. Finally, she pushed the laptop toward him. "It's the booking software for the inn. It's been glitching all week. Keeps freezing when I try to pull up reservations. I've tried everything I can think of."

Donald pulled the laptop closer, studying the screen. "Old-school system. Let me guess, you haven't updated the software or your subscription in a while?"

She shot him a look. "Do you know how much those updates cost?"

"Fair point." Donald nodded, typing quickly. "But you're in luck. I know a workaround."

Deborah crossed her arms again. He noticed the plump perk of her breast as she said, "And why would you help me? Don't you have a family to swindle or something?"

He paused, his fingers hovering over the keys. "Wow. You really don't hold back, do you?"

Deborah shrugged. "Call it how I see it."

Donald shook his head with a chuckle. "Maybe I just like solving problems."

"Or creating them," she muttered under her breath.

Ignoring her jab, Donald continued typing. After a few minutes, the system rebooted, and the reservation screen loaded smoothly.

"And…voilà," he said, turning the laptop back toward her.

Deborah leaned in, testing the system. It worked seamlessly. She raised her eyebrows, impressed despite herself.

"How'd you do that?"

"Just needed to clear the cache and update the drivers," he said casually.

She gave him a long look. "You have a reputation for being a lot of things, Donald Potter, but I didn't expect 'tech wizard' to be one of them."

"See? I'm full of surprises," he said with a laugh. He took a deep breath, filling his chest. His signature confidence radiating as Deborah Jackson thanked him again.

"How about I cover the cost of your dinner tonight as a thank-you?"

"I appreciate the offer, but no need. It is a corporate expense. But, I tell you what—if you're up for a little fun challenge, there's something I'd much prefer."

Curiosity tilted her head. "Oh? What's that?"

"If you can tell me the ingredients for that EGO1, I'll pay you double for my dinner instead. I've had my share of exceptional Long Island Teas, but that? That's pretty remarkable and your mixer has been sworn to some fraternal secrecy."

Deborah raised an eyebrow, intrigued. "And if I'm not able to?"

Donald leaned in slightly, playfully. "Then you join me for dinner and tell me more about you, Brightmoor, and this Inn."

Feigning defeat, she crossed her arms and lets out a soft sigh, as though the weight of the challenge is too much. "You've got me there, Mr. Potter."

Donald cleared his throat, realizing he may have overstepped. "Forgive me. I travel a lot—too many cities, too many late nights—and sometimes forget the size of each market. You run a fine establishment here, and I'd still very much enjoy dinner with you. No liquor knowledge required."

She nodded, appreciating his recovery. "Excuse me," she said and nodded to the server. The young waitress returned to the table with Donald's meal and two tall cocktails. She paused mid-step, a mischievous spark lighting her young eyes. Deborah knew that smirk, "Go ahead, Kim, settle down." She laughed and sipped her drink. Kim pivoted and leaves Donald admiring the drink and meal. Deborah lifted her glass pretending to toast, smiling as though she held up a trumped-up spades hand.

"Delta Dirt Vodka and Gin, Striped Lion Rum, and T.W.F Tequila. That's the EGO1. I've done a little traveling myself, Mr. Potter."

Donald's mouth opens slightly in surprise before a wide grin spreads across his face. "Touché, Ms. Jackson. Touché."

Deborah closed the laptop and leaned back, studying him. "Alright." She said sipping her drink. For a moment she enjoyed its flavor and the Temptations upbeat version of *Rudolf the Red-Nosed Reindeer* playing through the Inn. "Now. Mr. Potter. Why are you really here? And don't give me the corporate pitch." She placed her drink gently on the table. The elixir relaxed her.

Donald hesitated, for once, he was unsure of how to say what he was being compelled to say. "Honestly? Ms. Jackson, It's my job." He ate a spoon of the cornbread dressing mixed with fresh greens, then sipped the EGO1. "I'm good at it. And I gueeesss…" He trailed off, looking at her. "Well, I know I am helping families. These depositions and cash offers and development acquisitions actually help the living descendants of these families. I mean it is a, a benefit ultimately—"

"Ultimately?" Deborah tilted her head. "And now? That doesn't sound convincing."

He shrugged. "After dealing with the Richardson family and a few others since the pandemic. Now, I'm not so sure." His vulnerability surprised him.

Her expression softened. "Well, maybe you should figure that out before you make any more deals especially during the holidays and especially among my friends in Brightmoor."

Donald nodded slowly. "Maybe."

For the first time since joining RAXY's executive team, Donald felt something unfamiliar tugging at him—a desire to understand, rather than just close a deal.

~~ ~~

The next morning, Myles stood on the porch, enjoying the morning air crisp against his skin. He sipped warm lemon water, watching as the sun broke through the fog, casting a golden light over the fields. Inside, the living room was transformed into a makeshift war room, including a break table of paninis, tāst coffee, and fruit bowls from Brightmoor Inn.

Malcolm Wesley arrived carrying a stack of binders and a laptop. Aaron prepared the television for presentation of the drone footage, and Kent ensured the elders were comfortable for a long day in their recliners. The family gathered their expressions a mix of curiosity. Malcolm took his place at the head of the room, his commanding presence settling the group. For the next seven or eight hours, the Richardson homestead would be abuzz as the family prepared for a final meeting with Malcolm Wesley and Mission More's financial partners. Malcolm arranged for attorney Tina Bell of Jacksonville, Florida, to be on standby if the family needed quick, thorough legal advice.

"Good morning, everyone," Malcolm began, his tone warm and focused. "I know the last five days have been pretty intense and your questions and even some trepidation have increased, but I want to start by saying this: you are in a remarkable position with several options. Let's start with the documents Carolyn and CeCe Dupree found last week. They give us a stronger foundation than we initially thought."

Diane's lawyer instincts engaged. "You're talking about the legal agreement, right? Is there a loophole?"

Malcolm handed a copy of the documents to Diane, first, then to the others. "The legal agreement which is dated 1933 stipulates that any sale or transfer of ownership must be approved unanimously by all primary heirs. It is the binding document of record for this property and for all the primary heirs. Without their consensus, RAXY's claim is legally weak, possibly invalid, and predatory."

Grand Uncle Philip let out a low whistle. "You mean we've got a fighting chance?"

"More than that," Malcolm said, his confidence palpable. "We can file an injunction to stop RAXY from further action until this is sorted in court. But there's a catch."

A murmur rippled through the room. "What kind of catch?" Grand Aunt Sharon asked, her piercing gaze fixed on Malcolm.

"We need every living heir to agree to this plan," Malcolm explained. "No dissenters, no holdouts. If even one person sides with RAXY, it could jeopardize our strategy."

The room grew tense. Myles exchanged glances with Carolyn. Grand Aunt Sharon reached for her notepad and began writing.

"So, is there a purchasing alternative?" Tara, the real estate agent, crossed her arms. "And if we don't find these primary heirs, what happens?"

"I'm not a property preservation attorney like Tina which is why she is a partner in this endeavor, but, RAXY Corporation may be able to eventually take partial or full ownership. Time and greed are on their side," Malcolm said bluntly. "And they'll develop this land into something unrecognizable—likely pushing out the very community it's meant to serve."

The gravity of his words settled over the group like a heavy fog. Malcolm took a deep breath and stood next to Grand Uncle Philip. "This land isn't just yours. With all due respect. It is a part of Brightmoor's and Alabama's history."

"Yes," Myles stood quickly. "If we lose it, we lose a piece of ourselves. I know everyone doesn't see it the same way, but I'm asking you—no, I'm begging you, Richardsons—let's stand together on this." He pointed to the documents on the table.

Carolyn watched proudly. Myles wasn't just fighting for the land; he was fighting for the family's soul.

"You've got my support, Myles." Grand Aunt Sharon voice was resolute.

"Mine too." Grand Uncle Philip nodded slowly, reaching to shake his grandnephew's hand.

Diane tapped her pen against the binder, deep in thought. Lonnie stood behind her, understanding his role as a confidant. "Legally, this makes sense. I'm saying, 'yes.'" She said. Phylicia studied her bowl of fruit, whispering concerns with Kent who seemed to reassure her by holding her hand. She nodded in agreement.

Tara hesitated, her gaze shifted from the group to the photographs on the wall. Finally, she sighed. "Alright. I'll back it—but only because you all believe in it so much."

Laina, Aaron, and Aunt Nadine said "Yes" unsure of their need to vote.

Relief washed over the room, then Grand Aunt Sharon handed her notepad to Myles. "Here's a list of the living Richardsons and their county last I remember, son. I don't trust my handwriting but my mind is mighty sharp. You better get busy. We only have a few more days."

Myles knew the real challenge lay ahead.

Convincing the estranged members of the family—some of whom hadn't stepped foot on the land in decades—would be no easy task.

In the days that followed, the Richardson family sprang into action. Myles and Malcolm worked tirelessly to identify and contact the remaining heirs. Carolyn joined the effort, her natural charisma proving invaluable in bridging gaps and easing tensions.

~~ ~~

Myles invited Tara to ride to Savannah, Georgia, to meet with Grand Aunt Lorraine, a spirited woman in her late seventies who had distanced herself from the family years ago. Her quaint house was filled with the aroma of baked goods, and she greeted them with a wary but curious smile.

"So," Grand Aunt Lorraine said, settling into a floral armchair, "what brings you two all the way out here? Don't tell me Sharon finally decided to apologize for stealing my sweet potato pie recipe."

Tara chuckled, quickly seeing herself in her elder aunt. "If she hasn't by now, I doubt she ever will."

Sitting near his grandmother's twin, Myles leaned forward. His tone earnest. "We need your help, Aunt Lorraine. The family land is in trouble, and we can't save it without you."

Grand Aunt Lorraine's eyes showed her stern skepticism. "Without me?! I've heard that song before. What makes this time any different?"

"A few things makes this time different, Auntie Lo." Tara took over, her voice steady and persuasive. Myles was proud his discernment said Tara would be the perfect partner for this meeting. She called her aunt an endearing name he knew she hadn't heard in at least thirty years. "Aunt Lo, for starters, we are back together. All of the Richardsons are at the house deep in Genwea Crossing and we are all in agreement to make this family whole." Their eyes locked. Tara was obviously the daughter Aunt Lorraine never had. "And! Because this isn't just about the land. It's about preserving a legacy. If we don't act now, the next generation won't have the same opportunities or memories we did. Myles is leading this charge, and I can promise you, he's not giving up without a fight. He's liable to sit here with you for the rest of the year if he has to!"

Grand Aunt Lorraine studied them for a long moment, then sighed. "What do you want me to do, Chile?"

"Just say you agree to hold the land in the Richardson Trust and not sell." Tara offered quickly as Myles chose to allow his cousin to lead the way.

"Alright. Count me in." She said, reaching for a pen to sign the paper Tara and Tina prepared. "But if Sharon trifling behind so much as mentions that pie recipe, I'm out!"

Tara laughed, "Yes ma'am."

"And please get me a copy of Cousin Mamie's pound cake recipe. My Lord, that's some good eating!" She rocked a little in the chair as they continued catching her up on everyone who was at the house. When Myles and Tara got back in the car, the radio clicked on *Sleigh Ride,* and Tara—a consummate dancer and choreographer—couldn't resist singing along with T.L.C. "Let's have a very merry Christmas and a Happy New Year," she sang.

"I see someone is getting in the Christmas spirit," Myles teased.

"I love the music, Cousin, you know that." She admitted. "I just hate the stress of unpacking, decorating, buying the perfect gift for imperfect people, cooking, entertaining, and cleaning up, I was an only child and this crap is exhausting." She hummed more.

As he drove back to Brightmoor, Myles admired her. "You have a way with people."

She shrugged, a playful smile tugging at her lips. "I just know how to sweet-talk stubborn relatives. It's a Richardson skill."

Meanwhile, Aunt Nadine, Phylicia, Laina, and Aaron organized what they called a family caravan and drove throughout Macon County to locate cousins Horace, Alphonso, and Darius.

And, Malcolm, Carolyn, and Diane dug deeper into RAXY's corporate files, uncovering a pattern of questionable practices not only there in Brightmoor but across Alabama's original Black farm land. Armed with this information, they prepared to file an injunction.

~~ ~~

The house was unusually quiet. The day's efforts of rallying support and making calls to distant family members had drained everyone. Myles and Carolyn sat on the front porch steps, a shared blanket draped over their legs to ward off the night's chill. A lantern flickered beside them, casting a warm glow on their faces. Myles leaned back on his elbows, looking up at the clear sky. Carolyn Dupree had become his secret weapon and thought partner—again. Her intellectual athleticism was as fierce as any championship strategies she executed on the basketball courts.

As they sat under a blanket of stars, Myles turned to her. "Carolyn, I know you've been facing your own decisions about your career and about Brightmoor, I just want to thank you for taking on this work with me. You are amazing," his voice low and sincere. He was tired yet energized.

Carolyn met his gaze, "You're not alone in this, Myles."

Their eyes held the moment, until they heard branches shifting beyond the garden.

"I bet that was our first Christmas deer," Myles said.

"Yes, that would be good luck," Carolyn sat in the symbolic moment certain that Myles had overlooked the deer's presence meant creativity, resourcefulness and knowledge, while representing safe journeying and endurance through travels. Carolyn sipped a hot toddy.

"You know," he said, "I used to come out here as a kid and count the stars. I'd think about what life would look like out there —bigger, shinier. Today, all I want is to keep my feet planted right here."

She glanced at him. "It's funny how life works, isn't it? Sometimes we chase the horizon only to realize the treasure was under our feet all along."

Myles turned to her, his gaze lingering. "Speaking of treasures. You've been one through all of this."

Carolyn raised an eyebrow, a teasing smile playing on her lips. "Careful, Myles Richardson. Are you trying to charm me?" She pushed against his shoulder.

"Maybe I am." He grinned. The sincerity in his tone cut through the playfulness. "You didn't have to stay and help. You've got a big life, and larger goals. But, you've been here every step of the way, discovering missing links to break RAXY."

Carolyn set her mug down. "Myles, this isn't just your fight. It's ours. What happens to this land affects the whole community. And... well, maybe I see more in you than just a man fighting against a big corporation."

"More, huh?" His eyes searched hers, and for a moment, the weight of unspoken feelings hung within him. Like what?"

"Like someone who has the strength to carry his family, even when he's tired. Someone who sees value in things most people overlook." She paused, brushing a strand of hair from her face. "And someone who makes me believe in a realm of possibilities I hadn't considered before."

Myles waited. When she didn't continue, he leaned closer smelling remnants of her 4R perfume nearly at a loss for words. His voice dropped to a whisper. His hand brushed hers, tentative but firm. "Carolyn, I don't know where this is headed—this fight, this land, us—but I know I don't want to face any of it without you."

Her breath caught. "You won't have to," she murmured.

The gap between them closed as he tilted his head toward her. Their kiss was gentle, unhurried, a promise in the making under the blanket of stars.

After a moment, they leaned apart, their hands still intertwined. "I've been thinking a lot about what Malcolm has been saying," Myles said. "About turning this place into something that can actually generate wealth for everyone."

Carolyn nodded, pulling the blanket tighter around her shoulders. It was nearing her bedtime. "Heirs' property is complicated, but Mission More has shown us it doesn't have to be a dead end. Have you thought about how you could structure the land differently?"

"Malcolm laid out a few options," Myles said. "Right now, the land is vulnerable because it's held in common ownership by all the heirs based on an ancient legal agreement. That's why RAXY thinks they can swoop in and take control. But if we convert it into a family trust or an L.L.C, we'd have more, undeniable legal protections."

Carolyn tilted her head, considering. "And those structures could also make it easier to raise funds, right? Like getting loans to improve the land or even attract investors."

"Exactly," Myles said, his enthusiasm growing. "And then there's the development side. Instead of selling off parcels piecemeal, we could think bigger. Malcolm mentioned options like creating a co-operative farming operation or leasing some of the land for renewable energy projects like solar farms."

Carolyn's eyes lit up. "Solar farms would tie in perfectly with the Chiuta. You'd not only generate income but also align with the community's values of sustainability."

Myles squeezed her hand. He hadn't told her about Chiutas and was impressed by her insight. "And it doesn't stop there. We could also develop part of the land for affordable housing or community spaces. The key is keeping control so that whatever happens benefits everyone—not just a few people and definitely not RAXY."

Carolyn smiled. "You've got the heart of a visionary, Myles. Turning something fragile into something enduring—that's how you will build generational wealth for the Richardsons."

He looked at her again. "I can't do it without you, Carolyn. Having your brain and beauty connected to this." He paused. "I'm starting to believe we can do this—not just save the land but build something better for Brightmoor."

She rested her head on his shoulder, the two of them gazing out at the land that held so much history and promise. "We can do this," she said softly. "Together."

~~ ~~

For a change in scenery, Carolyn asked Myles to meet her at the high school track at dawn. She needed to run and think and he needed to watch her run and think like they'd done so many times as college friends, attempting to coach each other through life. After forty minutes, they left the track and agreed to meet for brunch at the Brightmoor Cafe.

Kim entered the small room Myles had reserved for his meeting with Carolyn. She placed a fresh pot of coffee on the table. As she turned down Mary J. Blige's sultry version of *Have Your Self a Merry Christmas,* Carolyn walked in.

"Merry Christmas, Coach," Kim said, noticing how Carolyn looked more pensive than she did days ago. "I have a spinach quiche and a fruit smoothie with your name on it," she offered. "I'll go get it. Let me know if you need anything else."

"Thank you Kim, and tell your mother I said 'hello'."

With her free hand, Carolyn rubbed Myles shoulder and sat across from him. His laptop open between them. Stacks of papers covered the midsized table: old deeds, family records, photographs, plat maps, and notes from Mission More's research. The faint chirp of birds outside the window was a reminder of the peacefulness they were fighting to preserve. Their chatter and flusters covered Johnny Gill's demeaning love on Christmas Day.

Kim returned with brunch and gave Carolyn a quick hug, "Welcome back." She whispered.

Myles unrolled a survey map that covered half the table. "I reached out to Malcolm again last night and he sent over a few templates for structuring a family trust. It seems like the most straightforward option to protect the land."

Carolyn leaned over the map, tracing her finger along the property's boundaries. She noticed Dupree land on the west boarder of the Richardson, edging off the map.

"A family trust would mean the land stays together, but I'd need to establish clear rules about decision-making and profits. Everyone has to agree—especially the distant cousins who haven't been involved until now," he spoke quickly.

Carolyn placed a hand on his arm. Her touch grounded him. "Myles, You—of all people— can make them see the bigger picture. Once they understand how much value this land can generate over time, they would change their minds. I know you are already planning to hold a family meeting to lay it all out, but honestly, the way you all have been working together I really don't think the Richardsons will have a problem."

"Yeah," he said, his voice heavy with uncertainty. "But it's more than just convincing them. We need a plan that shows exactly how this land can generate wealth, not just for now but for the next generation, too."

"I only want you to be realistic about the short and long game, Myles. Thinking about the championship doesn't help you win the season." She said eating her quiche before opening a folder labeled "Richardson's Development Strategies for Generational Wealth."

"Let's get at it." She chuckled and pulled out a few pages.

"I've been researching ways to maximize the land's potential. Here are a few ideas," Myles said.

First on the list were "Agriculture Cooperatives". He pointed to the eastern section of the map. "This area is perfect for expanding sustainable farming operations. We could turn it into a co-op and family members can share in the profits while employing people here. Plus, grants for sustainable agriculture are abundant right now."

He took a green marker and circled the fields illustrated near the property line. These would allow for renewable energy projects. Leasing a portion for a solar farm would provide consistent income without requiring much maintenance. It aligns with the Chiutas, and we could partner with local organizations to bring energy back into the community." Carolyn knew Myles had studied urban planning and development but she did not recognize the depth of his knowledge until that moment. While he talked she poured him a cup of warm lemon water.

"You mentioned affordable Housing Development the other night. Explain more on that," she said offering him the water. His eyes widened. "This stretch near the main road could be developed into affordable housing. Our L.L.C could work with nonprofits or community development organizations to create homes for families. The land stays legal, and we would generate lease income."

He walked around the table just in time to notice a cafe patron walk past the glass door.

Donald Potter.

With every muscle in him, Myles restrained the urge to confront him.

"Myles. Myles!" Carolyn tensed her voice without yelling, "Myles Richardson!"

He turned quickly and looked at Carolyn. He shook his head, "I'm good," He said. "I'm good".

Carolyn gave him a minute as he watched Donald exit the cafe.

"Come back." She demanded. "Myles, what's next?"

The other options are pretty low hanging fruit. It's offering community event spaces like Malcolm Wesley's family is doing out in Tuskegee."

"I agree." She said, "People are always looking for rustic, picturesque spaces, and it would tie the family even more into the community in a meaningful way."

"And the last opportunity would be timber and land management," Myles said. Carolyn's face questioned the concept. "Selective harvesting of timber from the wooded areas could preserve the environment and bring income. It could even work with the event space for eco-tourism or even agro-tourism. Hell, Alabama's agritourism industry generated $9.84 million in income."

Carolyn was awestruck. "You've really thought this through, haven't you?"

Myles shrugged. "It's not just me. These are ideas we've seen work in other communities. But the key is getting everyone on the same page." He paced around the small room and swung his arms, stretching his limber back. His determination returned. "This will show everyone that the land is worth more than any check from RAXY. We just need to be transparent about the numbers and clear about how decisions will be made."

"Yes, sir, that's the short game. And it continues tonight, right? Aren't your remaining cousins driving in to sign off?" Myles nodded. He loved how her mind was already racing ahead.

"Mission More has offered the professional help for validating the original legal agreement, and Tara and Diane are working on preparing another appraisal of the land's value. I'd only want to add value for these potential uses and share details that way no one feels shortchanged."

Myles reached across the table, his hand covered hers. "Carolyn, I don't know how I got lucky enough to have you in my corner, but I'm not letting go. You're as much a part of this as everyone else, now."

"I knew I would find you two in here," CeCe said. She and Tara burst through the door. Myles released Carolyn's hands, "What's the drama for, ladies?" She said. Tara place a hot pecan pie on the table. "We had a little issue over at the house while you were away."

"Oh my," Myles said.

"But you know I handled it as only a valedictorian could, right?" Tara laughed.

"What happened," Carolyn asked.

"We were nearly in big trouble until I decided to look at who has been paying the property taxes all these years. And guess who it's been." She waited. "Seriously, guess."

"Who, Tara? Grand Uncle Phillip? Aunt Florence?" Myles guessed.

"No, sir," Tara grinned. "Auntie Lo!"

"What?!" Myles exclaimed.

"Yes, when she graduated from high school—as a top scholar mind you—Granddaddy Feshane took her to open a bank account with Freedman's Liberty and Trust and taught her to pay the taxes every year on his birthday and she has been doing so for damn near sixty years!"

"Wow!" Myles said.

"Yep! Grand Aunt Lorraine saved the day, and I cant wait to tell Grand Aunt Sharon"

"Is that who's gotten you in a festive spirit this year," CeCe asked, pointing at Tara's red and green sweater that boasted: *I'm on the Naughty List with No Regrets.*

"Myles, why don't you and Carolyn finish this over at our house. We've been trapped with the Richardsons for nearly two weeks. Let my sister breathe, Brother." CeCe teased.

They agreed.

At the Dupree's house, Myles and Carolyn worked tirelessly to prepare for the next family meeting on Christmas Eve Eve. Just like when they were younger, Carolyn left Myles working on the couch while she bathed and threw on the largest pajama set her slim frame could wear. She sat comfortably with her feet in the couch smelling like pure bliss. Myles quickly shifted his body away from her while they worked.

They created a detailed presentation, complete with visuals of the proposed projects and a breakdown of how each one could generate income. They practiced explaining the legal benefits of a family trust, emphasizing how it would prevent disputes and protect the land for future generations. They made sure that video conferencing was set up properly and rehearsed the online presentation several times to check for problems. Not only did he want each family member to agree to establish a trust and not sale any portion of the land, Myles was insistent on taking the task to completion.

~~ ~~

Donald enjoyed two EGO1s before drifting to sleep. He was startled in his room and his eyes opened. He glanced at the clock on the nightstand: 1:00 a.m. The night was unnervingly quiet, the kind of silence that seemed to hum with anticipation. As he rolled over, a soft light flickered near the window.

"Must be the streetlights," he muttered, closing his eyes again.

"Streetlights? Hardly," said a voice in the darkness.

Donald sat up abruptly, his breath catching in his throat. A figure, cloaked in a soft golden glow, stood at the foot of his bed. It was an older man dressed in a faded dated suit, his posture regal yet approachable.

"Who— Who are you?" Donald stammered.

"I am the Ghost of What Was and Is," the binary voice said calmly, adjusting it's lapel. "I've come to show you truths."

Donald frowned. "I don't have time for this. Whatever this is, it's some weird dream remnants of my second EGO1."

The ghost chuckled. "Oh, life can be a good or bad dream. But I won't waste your time. Come with me."

Before Donald could protest, the room melted away, replaced by the living room of a modest house. He recognized it instantly—it was his childhood home. The threadbare couch, the tiny Christmas tree decorated with handmade ornaments, and the smell of cornbread in the air brought a rush to his chest.

The ghost gestured toward the kitchen. "Your mother. Do you see her?"

Donald's eyes followed, landing on his younger self sitting at the table, bent over a math book. His mother stood nearby, her hand resting on his shoulder.

"She worked two jobs, Donald," the ghost said. "She sacrificed sleep, health, and happiness to keep a roof over your head and food on this table. She didn't just work hard—she carried you on her back."

Donald's throat tightened as he watched his mother kiss the top of his younger self's head and whisper, "You're going to make it, baby. You're going to be something great."

"I know she worked hard," Donald said defensively. "But I put in the work, too. I studied that math book during the break to be prepared for my next class."

"Yes, you did. Did you steal that math book?"

Donald replied, "Of course I did not steal it, Ms. Riley gave it to me. She gave me free tutoring lessons and told me I could keep the book."

"Hmmmm. Let me show you more."

The scene shifted again. Donald found himself in a high school gymnasium. He saw a younger version of himself on the basketball court, surrounded by teammates. Coach Jones stood in the corner, hands on hips, shouting encouragement.

"Your coach paid for your shoes when your mother couldn't afford them. And he wrote your first recommendation letter for college."

The gymnasium faded, replaced by a fraternity house on a college campus. A group of young men wearing matching jackets surrounded him, clapping and chanting.

"These brothers covered your tuition when you were short," the ghost explained. "And they taught you the power of a network—a network you use to this day."

Scene after scene unfolded before him: His math teacher in seventh grade, staying late to tutor him; a cousin loaning him a car to get to his first internship; then, a senior deacon tailoring his first suit for a military interview.

By the end, Donald stood in the glow of the ghost's presence, tears burning his eyes.

"You didn't pull yourself up by your bootstraps, Donald," the ghost said softly. "You were handed boots—over and over again—by people who believed in you."

Donald's voice trembled. "Why are you showing me this?"

"To show you the truth," the ghost faded into a soft light. "No one makes it alone."

Slowly, through a purple haze, Donald's room reappeared, though he had little time to catch his breath before another presence filled the space. A nephilim stood in the corner shrouded in a silvery mist.

"And you?" Donald asked, weary. "Who? Are? You?"

"I am the Ghost of What May or May Not Be," it replied. Their voice echoing as though from a great distance. "I will show you the consequences of your actions."

Donald blinked, and the room dissolved.

Donald stood on the edge of a barren field. Rusted machinery dotted the landscape, and a small, dilapidated house sagged in the distance.

"What is this?" he asked.

"A family's legacy, lost," the ghost said. "This land once belonged to the Hamiltons. They trusted a man like you, who convinced them to sell. Now the land is stripped, and the family has nothing to show for it."

The scene shifted. A courtroom came into focus. A man in handcuffs was being led away, tears streaming down his face.

"That Black man you see is Robert Freeman Franklin. He fought to keep his family's land and was framed for a crime he didn't commit. Do you see the devastation, Donald? Land isn't just property—it's history, it's stability, it's hope."

Donald turned away, his heart pounding. "I didn't cause this."

"Perhaps not," the ghost said. "But you are part of the system that does. And yet..."

The mist around them shifted. Now, Donald stood in the center of a thriving farm. Children ran between houses, rows of crops, and solar panels laughing.

"This is what can be," the ghost said. "You have the power to transform heir property into generational wealth. Instead of taking, you can help families retain and build on what is rightfully theirs. Imagine creating more wealth, more love, more hope."

Donald's chest tightened as he looked at the vibrant scene. "How?" he whispered.

"By changing your purpose," the ghost said. "Your skills, your knowledge, your influence—they could heal instead of harm."

Donald turned to the ghost, but it was already fading. "Wait! What should I do?"

The ghost's voice echoed as it disappeared. "The truth is within you. Choose wisely."

Donald awoke with a start, his room dark and silent. His heart raced as he sat up, his mind swirling with images of the past and future. For the first time in years, he felt a crack in the armor he'd built around himself.

Is he part of something greater?

~~ ~~

Thanks to Lonnie and Kent, the old barn was transformed into a beautiful gathering space. Folding chairs and worktables formed a half-circle and. faced a projector screen. A sorting table against the back wall held warm refreshments. One-by-one, Richardson primary heirs, family members and their spouses trickled into the barn while others showed up online—all intrigued by Myles's and Mission More's promise of something greater.

Myles stood to address the group. "This land isn't just farmland," he began. Passion heaved his voice. "It's the Richardsons history, our legacy, and our present opportunity to build something that outlasts each of us. Today, we're going to show you how we can turn this into generational wealth—together." Everyone turned to the screen to watch the presentation. Save for the occasional creak of the barn's wooden beams, the barn was otherwise silent.

Myles took a deep breath and watched the faces of his family, noting how skepticism shifted to hope. The presentation ended with a slide featuring Aaron's drone footage and a montage of letters that stopped to form the phrase *Preserve Our Legacy, Build Our Future*.

Everyone remained silent, each having a varied emotion from curiosity, dubiety, and even excitement.

"I respect what you're trying to do, Myles," Aunt Nadine said, while standing up from her chair at the front table. Her tone measured. Grand Aunt Lorraine was the unofficial family historian, known for her sharp memory and even sharper tongue. She folded her arms and looked directly at Myles. "But some of us have been holding onto this land for years, paying taxes and keeping it up while others stayed away. How do we know this trust idea won't just tie our hands? And what about those of us who might need to cash out for our own families?"

Myles nodded, as though he had been waiting for the question. "Yes, ma'am. Thank you for asking that question and thank you even more for paying the property taxes for more than sixty years without our knowledge or support. We appreciate you. Your consistent financial management is one of the main reasons we are able to even have this conversation. Thank you."

He took a pause as the family cheered for her. "Yeah, Auntie Lo!" Tara shouted.

"I understand where you're coming from. I've asked our new financiers to help us devise a way to fairly and quickly repay you for the taxes you've paid as a major investment in every development we choose to make as a family."

To that, Grand Aunt Lorraine, smiled proudly and returned to her seat.

Myles continued, "The family trust will not tie anyone's hands. It is about creating a structure that ensures fairness beyond our lifetimes. If someone wants to sell their share, the trust can buy it from them at market value, keeping the land intact indefinitely. That way, no one is forced to stay, but the land doesn't get divided or sold to outside interests."

"Or taken by Wealth Strippers," Malcolm chimed in, his voice warm and firm. "And for those who commit to stay, the projects Myles has outlined—like the solar farm and community spaces— can generate income to cover taxes, maintenance, and even dividends for all members. It's about creating options and stability, not limitations."

Cousin Darius raised his hand. "I like the idea of making money off the land, but what happens if these projects fail? Do we all go broke?"

"That's a fair concern," Myles said, addressing the former football star directly. "That's why we'll start small. The solar farm, for example, is low-risk because you will lease the land to a company that manages the operations. We'll have guaranteed income from the lease without any of the Richardsons having to put up our own money. As for the other projects, like the tree harvesting and Chiuta, we will roll them out gradually and only after thorough feasibility studies."

Cousin Horace, leaned against the cane resting on his knee. "It sounds good on paper, but what happens when there's a disagreement? Families fight, and I don't want to see this land get torn apart because of bad blood. Hell, We have some folk still arguing over pie and pound cake recipes!"

"That's why the trust would be established. The legalities and federal regulations of having a trust come with clear rules," Myles replied. "We'll establish a family council—representatives from different branches of the family—to make major decisions. And if there's ever a deadlock, we can bring in a neutral third party, like a mediator, to resolve disputes."

"Like the Mafia?" Twelve-year-old Alphonso shouted. Everyone chuckled and Myles responded, "Yes Al, like the Mafia."

"We still have time tonight to answer questions, but on the tables are affidavits for your signature, saying you agree to the trust or you would like to sell your shares directly to the Richardson heirs during this holiday. The family members began whispering to one another. Some nodded in agreement, while others furrowed their brows in thought. It was clear that the presentation had planted seeds, but not everyone was ready to jump on board.

Then, unexpectedly, the smallest voice came from the back cutting through the noise. "I think this is brilliant!" Lela said, standing up, waving her signed paper. She was the youngest female cousin, home on semester break from Grambling State University. "We always talk about how we wish we had more opportunities back home. This plan could bring those opportunities—not just for us, but for the whole community. And isn't that what family's supposed to be about?"

Cousin Darius's stern expression softened, and even Cousin Horace gave a nod of approval.

Myles stepped outside of the barn. Phylicia was enjoying the crisp evening air which was a welcome contrast to the stuffy barn. She leaned against the barn wall, exhaling deeply. The musk of rotten hay, rusted oil cans, and sweet sugar cane overwhelmed her.

"Hey," he said, watching his sister take in deep breaths. Never one for conflict, he knew these two weeks were beyond her social battery life.

"Yeah," she said. "You laid everything out honestly, and you showed us the potential. That's all you can do. Now it's up to them."

"Thanks," he said. In his peripheral, he could see her hand rub uncomfortably across her stomach. "Are you?" He whispered in shock.

"SSHHH!," she laughed. "Yes. But Kent doesn't know yet. I'm trying to wait until Christmas but it's like holding a jackrabbit in my hips." Myles grabbed his sister and hugged her. "Merry Christmas. We have another heir."

"Don't tell!" She pleaded with Myles. Her mouth muffled by his bear hug.

When they re-entered the barn, Grand Aunt Lorraine stood at the front, acting again as the unofficial spokesperson. "We've talked it over," she said, glancing at the group behind her. "Not everyone's convinced yet, but most of us agree—it's worth a shot. On one condition: we want to be involved every step of the way."

Myles felt a surge of relief and gratitude. "That's exactly what we want. This is our family's land, and the only way this works is if we do it together."

She handed Myles thirteen signed affidavits. Myles promised to organize a workshop with a real estate attorney and financial advisor to finalize the legal structure and development plans.

~~ ~~

On Christmas Eve, Genwea Crossing was aglow with Christmas lights and fresh garland woven in crimson ribbons, and white, pine wreathes linking gates between the homes and wrapping trees of the intimate community. A drive down past the old Piggly Wiggly led directly to the door of Immaculate Conception Catholic Church where the youth ministry gathered singing carols and drinking hot coca—one of the few traditions remaining in Brightmoor.

To her surprise, Donald Potter sat in the grassed parking lot of the church nearby. He seemed solemn, in a daze, listening to the carolers. *Ole, rat. He needs a little Christmas spirit with all the ruckus he's* started. She thought, sounding more like her grandmother than herself.

After hugging most of the youth and their parents, she whispered a prayer of thanks for the wisdom to make the best decision of her life and to honor her parents. She drank warm, Golden Milk from her high school thermos, while humming en route to the Richardson's home.

The house was warm and full of laughter. And the smells of sweet desserts overwhelmed each guest. Grand Aunt Lorraine had prepared pies for every household and two fresh pound cakes sat in the center of the dessert table, surrounded by pecan candy, peppermint log. The Mclendon's Christmas album played throughout the house while Cousin Horace tinkered on the piano. The scent of pine mingled with the delicious aroma of holiday dishes, filling the air with nostalgia and cheer. The long farmhouse dinner table was crowded with plates loaded with ham, macaroni and cheese, candied yams, fresh snap beans, and other Southern staples. In the center of the table sat another golden, perfectly-baked pound cake. Its edges slightly crisp and its sugary glaze shined under the candlelight.

"Now, that pound cake is exactly how Cousin Mamie made 'em. Every slice tastes like heaven." Grand Uncle Phillip declared, pointing his fork at the dessert,

Everyone murmured in agreement, reaching for seconds—or thirds. Myles nodded appreciatively. "It's been on point every single time we've had it these past few days. Whoever's behind it, I salute you."

"I watched Cousin Mamie make her pound cake plenty of times. I even looked for her recipe, but it was nowhere to be found. I was sure it had been lost forever," Laina said. "Grand Aunt Nadine, would you please give me the recipe?"

She threw up her hands, laughing. "Don't look at me, Chile! I don't have Mamie's pound cake recipe either!"

The room fell silent, forks hovering mid-air. Carolyn exchanged curious glances with Myles, who raised an eyebrow.

Myles shook his head. "As far as I know, cakes have been here since the first night we all started sitting down to talk about the land. I assumed someone in the family was baking it. Come to think of it, Cousin Mamie's Early Rise tea is served over at the cafe now when you meet in the library."

"And it is so good," Diane admitted.

Between laughing and murmuring, they tried to figure out the mystery of the pound cake. Who made it? How had it arrived? It was as if the dessert had appeared out of thin air.

A loud knock echoed through the house, silencing the room. The sound was so unexpected that one of the younger children, a boy of about eight, instinctively ran to open the door before any of the adults could stop him. The child pulled the door wide, revealing Donald Potter standing on the porch, dressed impeccably in a tailored hunter green suit, a red ascot around his neck, and his polished shoes gleaming. He flashed a warm, smile and stepped inside as if he belonged.

"Well, good evening, everyone," he said, scanning the room.

The family froze, exchanging confused glances. Myles stepped forward, his brow furrowed, and crossed his arms. "Donald Potter. What are you doing here?"

"I'm here to discuss the land. Mamie invited me."

A wave of groans rippled through the room. Family members looked at one another, shocked.

Myles's eyes narrowed as he tilted his head. "Mamie invited you?"

"Yes," Donald said, his tone steady. "We've had a few conversations over tea, and she asked me to join the family gathering tonight. If you'd let me in the other day, I could've explained it —"

Interrupting, Myles took a hard step closer. His voice firm. "Donald, do you even know—"

Donald held up a hand, cutting him off. "Before you say anything, let me explain. I know how I must look to all of you, and I know what people think of me. A 'Wealth Stripper,' right? Someone who comes in, takes what doesn't belong to him, and leaves destruction in his wake."

"Absolutely," Myles replied.

The room went eerily quiet. Even the children sensed the tension and froze in place.

"I get it," Donald's voice was softer. "I've spent years convincing families like yours to sell their land. I believed I was helping them —helping them get money and opportunities quicker than they ever had. But what I didn't understand, until recently, is that this land is worth far more than money. It's a legacy, your legacy, and it shouldn't be sold. It should be protected, nurtured, and developed. And I wanted to let Mamie know she was one hundred percent correct."

The hushed conversations around the living room grew louder now, but this time they weren't voices of disbelief. They were questions, whispers of curiosity.

Donald took a step toward the center of the room. "When I met with Mamie at the library, something changed. She didn't just talk to me about the land; she talked to me about what it means. She told me stories about your family—about the sacrifices, the struggles, the victories that this land represents. And then, last night—" He hesitated, unsure how much to reveal.

"Last night, what?" Myles asked sharply.

Donald exhaled, gathering his thoughts. "Last night, I was visited by truths I couldn't ignore. Truths about my own life and about the lives of so many families like yours—and even my own. I realized that I've been blind. Blind to everything that really matters."

The older members of the family exchanged knowing looks. Laina crossed her arms, stepping up to move the younger child away from Donald. "So, what are you saying, Donald?"

"I'm saying that I was wrong," he said simply. "I thought I pulled myself up by my bootstraps, that no one helped me. But Mamie—and other truths I've come to see—made me realize that I had help every step of the way. My mother, my teachers, my coaches, my fraternity brothers—they all gave me the tools to succeed. And yet I've been part of a system that strips other families of their core, leaving them with nothing."

Donald paused, looking around the room. "I'm not here tonight to convince you to sell your land. I'm here to tell you not to."

Myles looked at Donald curiously.

"You really mean that?" Myles asked.

"I do," Donald said firmly. "I want to help you all keep this land. I've spent years learning the ins and outs of real estate, and I'm offering that knowledge to you. For starters, with the uninterrupted tax payments you all have made and now with Mamie not agreeing to sign away her portion, RAXY's lawyers are pinning for ways to nullify their offer to you all. Together, we can turn this land into generational wealth without selling it to anyone."

Grand Aunt Sharon walked slowly from the back bedroom where she often rested and prayed. "Mamie? Did you say Mamie told you all this?"

Donald nodded. "She opened my eyes to things I hadn't seen—or hadn't wanted to see. Even the tea she gave me tasted so divine. She believed that our people would do the right thing and do right by one another." Then Donald scanned the room, "Where is she? Has she should not arrived, yet?"

Myles raised a hand to quiet everyone. He turned to Donald, as a soft *plink* vibrated through the room. It sounded like a tuning fork traveling from room to room, stoning around the guests. Phylicia felt a warmth and grabbed Kent's hand. Everyone's eyes followed the invisible sound toward the Christmas tree, where an ornament had fallen to the wooden floor.

Myles walked to the tree. A fallen ornament glinted in the glow of the fireplace. He bent down and picked it up.

A hush fell over the room as Myles held the ornament in his hands. He turned it over carefully, reverently, his expression one of awe and realization.

It was Cousin Mamie's ornament—a delicate, handmade piece shaped like a small bundt pan, decorated with gold trim. On its side was her picture and name. Slowly, he placed the ornament back on the tree, his fingers trembling slightly. "I don't know what's going on, but I know one thing: we are being reminded of what family is about—and why this land matters."

Myles turned to face Donald.

"Donald," his voice measured, "there's something you need to know about Mamie."

Donald furrowed his brow. "What about her? She's been... gracious, and insightful. She's the one who helped me realize the importance of what you have here. Is she ok?"

Myles exchanged a glance with his family and then concentrated on Donald, "Donald, Mamie Ross has been gone for nearly five years. She passed away just before her ninety-fifth birthday."

The room grew so quiet that the only sound was the crackling of the fire. Donald's jaw tightened, his confusion deepening. "That's impossible. I... I spoke to her. We sat together in the back room at the library. She told me about her connection to this land, and about her dreams for it. How could she be... gone?"

Myles sighed, stepping closer to Donald. "Mamie loved the library. They even dedicated one of the rooms to her, naming it after her."

Donald shook his head. His voice trembled, "I know what I saw. I know what I heard. She called me by name. We drank tea. She told me stories about her childhood. She... she even gave me advice. How can that not be real?"

Myles placed an empathetic hand on Donald's arm. "Cousin Mamie was a wise woman. Her presence is still felt by many of us. It's not uncommon for people to feel like she's still watching over this family, this land. Maybe what you experienced wasn't just in your head. Maybe she was trying to guide you, to help you see something you couldn't before."

Donald sank into a nearby chair. The room swirled with the memories of his encounter with Mamie Ross—her gentle smile, her knowing eyes, her words that had pierced straight through his carefully constructed defenses.

"She said..." Donald began, his voice shaky. "She said the universe provides truth when you're open to it. That I needed to listen, to really see. She told me stories about her family's struggles, but she also talked about forgiveness. About redemption."

"That sounds exactly like Mamie!" Grand Uncle Phillip laughed.

"If Cousin Mamie's words changed your perspective, then maybe you've been given a second chance. But don't mistake that for an easy road, Donald," Diane said. "It's going to take more than a change of heart to earn people's trust—especially to earn this family's trust."

Donald looked up at the family. "I understand. And I want to honor Mrs. Mamie's legacy—and your family's. This land deserves to remain in your hands, only you can cultivate it into something remarkable."

They listened silently absorbing his words.

"If Mamie believed you deserved a second chance, then I think we should find it in our hearts to do the same, son," declared Grand Uncle Philip.

Cousin Horace knocked his cane against the door frame, "But actions, son. Actions will be what matters."

"I'll prove it," Donald said resolutely. "I'll do whatever it takes to show you that I'm serious."

Myles gave him a long, appraising look before finally nodding. "Alright. Let's see what you're made of Donald Potter."

The two men clasp hands, quickly offering their fraternal shake.

"Had I known you were frat, we would've gotten you straight two weeks ago," Myles jested, patting Donald on the back.

"Come on in and have dinner," Aaron offered, modeling his cousin's grandeur.Donald grappled with the truth of what had happened. Mamie Richardson Ross, gone yet somehow present, had opened his eyes to a new purpose. Now, it was up to him to walk the path. He silently vowed to honor the guidance she had given him, even if he couldn't fully understand how it had come to be. For the first time in years, Donald felt a flicker of something he hadn't allowed himself to feel: hope.

"Well, I don't know about y'all, but I'm cutting myself another slice of pound cake. If Cousin Mamie sent this cake down from heaven, I'm not letting it go to waste!" Aunt Nadine said, reigniting the family chatter though the mystery of the pound cake lingered in everyone's mind.

As they walked towards the kitchen and dining room, Deborah Jackson knocked on the door. She walked in with a smile. Myles walked to Deborah with a little amazement. She held out a small hand written invitation. It read, "Come join the Richardsons for a Christmas Eve celebration. Bring a cocktail."

It was signed *M.R.*

"Wooow!" Myles laughed. "The more the merrier!"

"I brought a bottle of EGO1 for you all to enjoy." She smiled, recognizing Donald. He returned a smile, then raised his eyes to the ceiling. He mouthed, *Thank you, Mamie.*

As they enjoyed the rest of the evening, they glanced at Cousin Mamie's ornament, feeling a quiet connection to Christmas magic, their past, the love of family, and the thrill of officially becoming heirs for the holiday.

Myles quietly walked over to Carolyn who stood by the tree, holding the ornament and quietly eavesdropping on Phylicia's plans to announce her pregnancy.

She beamed, longingly. On cue, Lonnie began singing The Temptations's *Silent Night,* matching Eddie Kendricks' falsetto voice perfectly. Then, Uncle Horace picked up Melvin Franklin's bass.

"Carolyn Dupree." Myles turned her to him. "What do you want? I'm asking nicely."

Carolyn turned to face him. Before she could respond, he continued, "I know there are moments I need and want. Moments I need and want with you. You are my desire. Brightmoor is my future."

She touched his chest as he spoke, "I want to be your Black Santa, your Christmas joy. I want you to put your arms around me and be supported."

His poetic demand surprised Carolyn.

He rubbed her arm and whispered, "Then, I want you to tell me what you want under your tree from me." He pulled her into his embrace. She reached her hand into her back pocket and handed him an Brightmoor High School ID, bearing her headshot, and the title *Head Coach*.

He smiled and cuffed her face, pulling her into a long kiss.

Epilogue

It was just past midnight, late Christmas Eve when Myles pulled his truck into the gravel driveway of Carolyn's tiny home. The modest structure, with its cedar siding and string lights framing the windows, exuded warmth against the chill in the night. The moon reflected against the door, and a breeze carried the faint hum of Christmas carols from the Dupree family's main house.

Myles cut the engine but made no move to open the door. His deep-set eyes were fixed on Carolyn, who sat beside him in the passenger seat. Her long legs tucked under her.

She turned to meet his gaze, her piercing eyes searched his face as though deciphering a secret.

"You're quiet," she said softly, her voice like the low hum of a jazz melody.

"Just thinking," he replied, his voice gravelly, filled with unspoken weight. "About tonight, about Mamie, about us, about more."

Carolyn tilted her head, a small smile curving her full lips. "Those are good thoughts."

Myles reached for her hand, his fingers enveloping hers. For a quiet moment, his calloused thumb traced slow circles against her palm. "You have this way of making me feel." He paused, searching for the right words. "I knew you existed but did not know how to connect. Now, it feels like you were crafted for me."

Her breath deepened. The air between them was charged, electric. Carolyn finally broke the silence, her voice a whisper. "Come inside."

Her words flowed through Myles and he felt himself growing in desire and his mouth watering with sweet anticipation. They stepped into her tiny house. The Christmas wreath adorning the door jingled as it closed. The warmth welcomed them. With two steps into the minimalist home, Myles stood in its center.

Her home was small but thoughtfully arranged. Bookshelves lined the top two feet of each wall, extending the width of the home, holding well-worn titles and framed basketball trading cards. A small, decorated tree twinkled in one corner.

Two unpacked moving boxes stacked against the wall. An emerald green oversized loveseat with a matching ottoman and decorative crocheted pillows swallowed the opposite space. Myles smiled at the small neon pothos hanging from miniature basket-ball goals nailed into the walls. An automatic air freshener, filled the room with a soft bergamot. He suddenly felt awkward in her intimate space. The sole lamp illuminated from the loft of the tiny home casting just enough light for them to see one another.

Carolyn gestured for him to take off his coat before sliding off her red jazzy fringe booties. She padded on bare feet across the cool, tiled floor. Her movements fluid and unhurried. His eyes never left her, taking in the way her cocoa-toned skin seemed to glow in the dim light, the way her high cheekbones and regal pos-ture made her look like she belonged in a portrait.

"Want some tea or pound cake?" she asked, already removing the glass cake cover. The sweet scent of cinnamon, nutmeg, and sugar tempted Myles. "No, thanks," he resisted.

His deep voice was soft.

She turned and caught him staring. "What?" she asked, a teas-ing smile playing on her lips. She was breathtaking.

"You," he said simply. "You are so much….Amazing."

Her smile loosened, replaced by something deeper, more vul-nerable. Slowly she crossed the small room to stand in front of him. Her amber eyes searched his face. "Myles," she paused, en-joying the strength of his name vibrating in her throat. "Myles, why did you really come here tonight?"

"Because you told me to come inside." His hand cradled her face. "Because I couldn't just drop you off and drive away. Not after tonight. Not after the impossible becoming possible, the supernatural natural, and the frequency that I felt. And your smile, your voice, your glow. I needed to be here—with you." He hesitated, but stood closer to her, "I need to be inside of you."

Carolyn's breath trembled as she leaned into his touch. "Show me."

Myles's right hand slid around her waist and pulled her closer until their foreheads touched. Their breath synced as the space between them disappeared. His lips touched hers tentatively, at first, then more insistent. He tasted her tongue, sweet and soft—just like his body knew her nipples would be. Her hands moved to his shoulders, sliding down to his chest. She felt the strength of his pectorals and its warmth. "I've been waiting for this, " she murmured against his lips. "...longing for you."

He released their embrace and looked into her eyes, "So have I, Carolyn Dupree," his voice was thick with love and lust. "You are my match." Her hands explored his face, tracing the sharp lines of his jaw and the softness of his goatee. Through his longing, he interpreted her touch as an invitation to explore her curves. Quietly, he marveled at the sensualness flowing over her feminine frame and how perfectly her body fit against his. Guided by an ancestral rhythm, they moved, embraced, against the wall. His kisses pleaded for more. She rubbed the side of the cabinet, and with quiet obedience, a Murphy Bed lowered. The palms of her hand lifted his shirt and his kiss on her shoulders lowered her dress. A universal frequency lit through them, sharing a warm energy that connected, vibrated, and multiplied. Their bodies exposed the truth of their admiration, every stroke revealed the language oneness. Each intimate touch etched their consummate love into their memory.

Myles lifted his body from her embrace, "You're staying in Brightmoor," he stated his question.

Carolyn nodded, "I am." Her touch against his bare chest released a sensation of light through his body. "Myles, I want to be here with you. To build something strong and unique. Something more." Tears glistened in her eyes, though she offered a simmering smile. "I've always seen you, Myles. Even through time and distance. And I will keep seeing you as long as you allow me."

Myles kissed her, capturing the sweetness of her promise while his heart offered his own. Time deepened as they melted into each other, their whispers, touches, and gazes knitted a patch quilt of love woven from years of private longing. Their kisses deepened; breaths mingled as their bodies explored the depth of their connection. Carolyn's essence discovered Myles's in ways no other woman had. He gripped her full roundness, sliding the pulse of his soul up her spine, strong and with intention. Her nails stabbed his skin and sent waves of heat coursing through the both of them. Their movements were natural and deliberate. Myles's lips traveled from her mouth to the curve of her neck down to her breast only stopping to admire.

"Delicious," He whispered. His tongue appreciated her tender nipples before enveloping into his mouth. Carolyn moaned, allowing her anticipation to welcome him knowing her, desiring her, and enjoying her. He kissed and sucked the length of her torso. He paused at her navel. Kissed her stomach just below and waited, quietly asking.

"Yes, please," Carolyn whispered. Her voice trembled. "I am yours."

Myles clinched her inner thighs and plunged kisses into her sweetness. He felt her body surrender to his satisfaction and what was once insatiable within him was matched as they gave themselves completely to one another. Their connection transcended physical lovemaking. It established their portal to pleasure and peace.

~~~~

As the first rays of Christmas morning sunlight filtered through the tiny house, their bodies still entwined, Myles brushed a strand of hair from Carolyn's face. His fingers lingering on her cheek. She looked up at him, her piercing eyes soft with emotion.

"Merry Christmas," she whispered.

He smiled, pressing a kiss on her forehead. "Merry Christmas, My Beautiful."

The warmth of their emerging love and the promise of more bonded them. Their lovemaking extended beyond friendship into sacred awe, and Heaven had approved.

www.ingramcontent.com/pod-product-compliance
Lightning Source LLC
Chambersburg PA
CBHW051310170626
46809CB00004B/1838